SEE

YOU

ON

THE

MAT

Happy Xmas Andy!
Love Jess, Lee, Bodhi + Arthur
x x

Happy Xmas Andy!

Love Jess, Lee,
Bodhi + Arthur
x x

SEE YOU ON THE MAT

A STORY OF PERSPECTIVE, RESILIENCE, AND TRANSFORMATION THROUGH BRAZILIAN JIU-JITSU

MARTY JOSEY

The following is a work of fiction. Characters, names, situations, events, and locations described are purely the invention of the author's mind, or are used fictitiously. Any resemblance to persons living or dead is purely coincidental.

All rights reserved. No part of this book may be used or reproduced in any manner whatsoever without written permission of the author.

See You on the Mat: A Story of Perspective, Resilience, and Transformation Through Brazilian Jiu-Jitsu
Copyright © 2020 Marty Josey

ISBN-13 979-8-67-143087-5

Independently published through Kindle Direct Publishing
https://KDP.Amazon.com

Cover and interior images © Scott Burr

Layout and cover design by Scott Burr
Connect with Scott online at www.EnclaveJiuJitsu.com

AUTHOR'S FOREWORD

I love Jiu-Jitsu. I've loved it since my first exposure to it. To be fair, I am passionate about martial arts in general, and have studied and trained various arts including Shōrin-ryū Karate, Tae Kwon Do, Kenpo Karate (Black belt), Progressive Fighting System / Contemporary Jeet Kune Do (PFS, Apprentice Instructor), Fear Adrenal Stress Response (F.A.S.T. Defense, Certified Instructor), Submission Grappling, et cetera.

I have trained martial arts for over thirty years, and—even though I've enjoyed many arts and styles—Jiu-Jitsu is my true love. Ever since my one and only year of high school wrestling (they cut the program my senior year), I've loved the grappling arts. My interest was reawakened many years after that year of high school wrestling when I saw the first UFCs in the early '90s. Watching Royce Gracie handle fighters from various backgrounds and styles and of various sizes was truly inspirational to me. It lit a fire within me and I knew I had to train Jiu-Jitsu. I started the journey by attending seminars, including weeklong seminars with Rickson Gracie (many hours away), and by purchasing the old Rorion Gracie VHS tapes. Unfortunately, there was nowhere to train consistently around me at that time. I dabbled a bit, but ended up doing other arts more consistently for several years, always knowing I'd return to Jiu-Jitsu someday.

In 2008, I started training Jiu-Jitsu consistently and never looked back. It has been, and continues to be, an incredible journey. My hope in writing this book is to spread the joy I've experienced through Jiu-Jitsu and to share the impact that Jiu-Jitsu can have on one's life, both on and off the mat.

Jiu-Jitsu is a brotherhood. I sincerely believe that. Through Jiu-Jitsu, we are all connected. It doesn't matter if you're a doctor, lawyer, construction worker, student, or stay-at-home mom, we are all one on the mat: we all want to grow, learn, progress, help, and become the best we can be. We all want to have fun, work hard, grow through challenges, and continue to move forward on our path.

This book is dedicated to all those who are making an impact, both on and off the mat.

M.J.
Durham, N.C.
2020

PREFACE

This book is about a journey: a journey of perspective. We all go through life with our own perceptions and expectations based on our pasts, our experiences, and our beliefs about how things are or how they should be. We interpret experiences and assign meanings to them. Many times the meanings we assign—and the perceptions we have based on them—are very limited. We project our preconceived notions onto situations, a tendency which oftentimes keeps us from fully understanding or appreciating the opportunities we have at our fingertips.

In this story you'll meet Spencer, a young man who thinks he knows how things are. But, as you'll see, he's about to find out that there is so much more to people and their situations than what's visible on the surface.

"Just when the caterpillar thought her life was over… she began to fly."

—Anonymous

Chapter
ONE

Thursday Night Training at Seleno BJJ

It was a hot and humid night at Seleno Brazilian Jiu-Jitsu. It had rained most of the day but now the rain had finally stopped, leaving the air thick and smothering. Class was set to start at 7:00 and by 6:50 most of the students had arrived and were getting some light stretching in on the mat. Others were just hanging out, talking and relaxing. It was a relaxed atmosphere, and everyone seemed happy to be there. At 6:55 a young man came through the door, hurried and stressed. He quickly made his way to the changing room and put on his gi. He hurried to the mat just before the instructor called everyone to line up. As a fairly new white belt, this student—Spencer—took his place in the back row. He seemed anxious about being in the class.

The class started with several minutes of warm ups, including standard Jiu-Jitsu movements such as shrimps, upas, forward and back rolls, and other movement drills. This was followed by some positional sparring drills to practice the material covered in the previous class. The instructor, Professor Alan Johnson, put a strong emphasis on positional sparring drills, because he believed that isolating parts of the whole was an effective way to develop a high level of skill in every position and scenario, compared to just covering a technique and then jumping into full rolling. This positional sparring was followed by a detailed technique breakdown. Tonight's technique was a Kimura flow from cross-side position. Professor spoke at length about the principles and concepts related to this position and flow, emphasizing that elements such as posture, pressure, and connection are more important than the technique mechanics themselves. He emphasized that it's these elements and concepts that make the technique come alive. The last part of class consisted of rolling, and Professor Johnson suggested that everyone pick something they wanted to work on during rolling and focus on that, instead of just "free-for-all wrestling."

During the rolling people were smiling, laughing, and sharing information. You could hear things like "Great job," "How did you do that," "Not this time brother, I'm on to that setup now," and, "You're getting so much better."

At the end of class, and after everyone had finished talking and visiting, Spencer walked with his head down and his shoulders slumped. Professor Johnson picked up on Spencer's demeanor and approached him.

"Hey Spencer, how's it going?"

"I'm OK."

Noticing the incongruity between Spencer's statement and his body language, Professor Johnson asked him, "Do you have time to talk for a few minutes?"

"Yeah, I guess," Spencer replied.

Professor Johnson led Spencer into his office and asked him to sit down.

"Mind if I ask what's going on with you?" Professor Johnson asked. "You seem kind of down... like you're not exactly having a great time in class."

Spencer was silent for a moment, holding his head down, and then looked up and said, "Yeah, I guess I don't get it. I don't get why things seem so easy for everyone else but not for me. I seem to be struggling all the time and it's so frustrating. This is the third BJJ school I've been to and it's always the same. Everyone seems to have it so easy, so effortless. And I'm not just talking about on the mat. I have so many things to deal with. I have so many problems and challenges in my life and it seems like everyone else is living a charmed life. Why do I have to struggle so much? Why do I have it so hard?"

Professor Johnson listened patiently and attentively as Spencer continued.

"What did I ever do to deserve all the hardship and struggle in my life? I feel like, if I didn't have so much to deal with, maybe I'd be picking up Jiu-Jitsu much better and easier. Why am I so cursed? I'm really starting to wonder if BJJ is for me. Like I said this is my third school, and it's always the same. I think I'm just going to quit. It's not like anyone would miss me if I wasn't here anyway. I think it's just too much."

Professor Johnson didn't jump right in, but instead let what Spencer had said stand for a moment. Then he looked into Spencer's eyes and said, "I can see that you're feeling frustrated, overwhelmed, and defeated."

Spencer nodded his head. Professor Johnson continued.

"Spencer, before you call it quits, would you be willing to do something for me? Would you be willing to participate in a little experiment?"

Spencer was intrigued by this request, and answered, "Yes, I guess. What do you have in mind?"

"Would you be willing to meet with some of the other students individually for a brief conversation about who they are and what led them to Jiu-Jitsu?" Professor Johnson asked. "I can arrange for it to happen this week."

Spencer thought for a moment and, though it made him feel somewhat uncomfortable, because he wondered if it meant they'd be "selling" him on the benefits of Jiu-Jitsu, he agreed.

"That's great, Spencer," said Professor Johnson. "I really appreciate your openness to doing this." He then got up and started walking towards the door. "Give me a minute," he said. "I'll be right back."

Spencer sat there wondering what he was actually getting himself into. After about five minutes Professor Johnson returned.

"OK," he said, "I just spoke with Michael, and he would love to meet you for coffee tomorrow morning. I know you are working as an Uber driver right now and looking for another job to supplement that. Write down your schedule for this week and I'll call you tomorrow with some days and times some of the other students can meet with you. Sound good?"

Reluctantly, Spencer said, "Yeah, that's fine."

"OK, Spencer," said Professor Johnson. "I'm really glad we were able to talk, and that you didn't just drop out of class without speaking to me first. I look forward to hearing about your experiences with the others."

With that, they said their goodbyes. Spencer walked out into the heavy night air, still feeling hopeless and defeated.

"Never limit the vision you have for your life based on your current circumstances or competencies."

—Brendon Burchard

Chapter
TWO

Michael
The Army Vet

The first person Spencer was going to meet was Michael, and they were to meet the following day. Spencer had heard that Michael was an Army vet, but that was all he knew about him. He was nervous about meeting Michael because he really had no idea what to expect. He was definitely out of his comfort zone, but, since Professor Johnson had asked him to do this, he was determined to see it through.

The next morning Spencer got dressed and drove to the coffee shop where Professor Johnson had arranged for them to meet, which was located just down the road from the Academy. He was still apprehensive about meeting Michael, and had to tell himself several times that it was going to be OK. He parked his car and walked into the coffee shop. He saw a man, sitting alone, who looked up and smiled at him as he walked in. The man got up and came over.

"Spencer?" he asked.

"Yes. Michael?" Spencer asked.

"Yes, I'm Michael. It's great to meet you."

They both sat down and Michael quickly said, "Thanks for agreeing to meet with me."

"No problem," Spencer replied. "I do have to admit, though, that I'm a little nervous about this whole thing."

"I can certainly understand that, Spencer," Michael said. "I can relate much more than you know with the anxiety of social situations. Let me share my story with you, and tell you about the role that Jiu-Jitsu has played in it. Spencer, want to know why I love Jiu-Jitsu?" Before Spencer could answer, he continued, "Because it's therapy for me. I mean, I do have an actual therapist and therapy has helped me a great deal, but I feel like I get a lot more out of Jiu-Jitsu. The endorphins that are released on a regular basis, the physical struggle of the "back and forth" of rolling, the surviving in and even becoming comfortable in bad positions and situations by remaining calm and breathing through it, have all made me more comfortable in my own skin again. This could only have been possible in an atmosphere of safety, trust, and acceptance. The camaraderie and support I've experienced in Jiu-Jitsu has had a profound impact on me—and I had a lot to overcome."

"Like what?" Spencer asked.

Michael explained: "I joined the Army right out of high school. I had always wanted to be a soldier and felt that it was my calling. After my initial training I went through Ranger School, and was assigned to the 75th Ranger Regiment. I loved being a part of special operations, and went on several missions over the next several years. Then I was sent to Afghanistan, and I really saw some heavy action. I don't like to go into detail about it, but I experienced some really shocking and traumatic things over there. It really messed me up. And when I say it messed me up, I mean it really messed me up... deep into my core. I knew I'd never be the same, and for a long time I contemplated suicide. I just couldn't get the horrific images out of my head. Some days I felt numb and couldn't feel anything, and other days I felt so much it was unbearable. It eventually ruined my relationship with my wife, and we split up, and it made it impossible for me to hold down a job. Ultimately, after many years in a downward spiral, I ended up homeless on the street. This was a very low point in my life. I cried privately every day during this time. I felt so hopeless. If it wasn't for Professor Johnson, there's no telling where I would've ended up."

"What do you mean?" asked Spencer.

"Well, one day I was lying on the ground, out cold. I had drunk myself into oblivion, like I did most days, and passed out. Professor Johnson saw me lying there and he noticed that my head was bleeding. I had apparently hit my head on a rock when I passed out. Professor Johnson called an ambulance and rode with me to the hospital. He waited there until I was treated, and when I was discharged he came and asked if I had anywhere to stay. I told him I did not, and he said that I could stay in the back room of the Academy. There was a cot there for me to sleep on. All he asked in return was that I help around the Academy—mopping the mats, cleaning the bathrooms, things like that—and that I attend Jiu-Jitsu classes. I couldn't believe his generosity. He literally saved my life. Helping out around the Academy and attending classes gave me something to do and, as silly as it sounds, it gave me a purpose. My world became about cleaning the Academy the best I could and soaking up all the knowledge I could during class. I started connecting with the other students, and I started feeling human again. Over time I started feeling better about myself. I did still struggle with PTSD, though, and Professor helped me find a therapist. It's been over four years now, and with the help of the therapist, the incredible connections I've made at the Academy, the stimulating learning experiences of BJJ, and the supportive atmosphere at the Academy, I can honestly say I've never felt better."

"Wow," Spencer said, "that's really great."

"Yes, it is Spencer," Michael said. "I eventually became a part-time instructor at the Academy, and I also work at the health food grocery store a couple of blocks from here. I also recently started giving back by working with other veterans, and my hope is to start a veterans-only class at the Academy. Professor Johnson is helping me plan it, and we hope to be able to offer it next month. I can't wait!"

"Wow," Spencer said again, "that's amazing. You've really turned your life around."

"Well," said Michael, "it never would have happened without Professor Johnson and the power of Jiu-Jitsu."

The two talked for a while longer, and then Spencer said he had to go.

"I really appreciate you sharing your story with me," he said.

Michael responded with, "My pleasure, Spencer. Anything I can do to help you, just let me know."

"Thank you," replied Spencer. "And, by the way, thanks for your service."

As he walked back to his car he replayed Michael's story in his head. It really resonated with him. Michael had overcome so much in his life, and it was inspiring to hear such a powerful story.

"Be thankful for the struggles you go through. They make you stronger and wiser. Don't let them break you. Let them make you."

—Anonymous

Chapter
THREE

Michelle

The next morning Spencer woke up feeling negative. He found himself thinking about the problems in his life. The more he thought about his problems the more overwhelmed he felt. He didn't even feel like getting out of bed. And then a funny thing happened: he thought about the conversation he'd had with Michael the day before. The more he played out the encounter, and what Michael had shared with him, the better he felt. He didn't really know why. *That's interesting*, he thought to himself. Then he jumped out of bed and headed for the shower.

The next person Spencer was to meet with was Michelle. They were to meet at the same coffee shop where he had met Michael. Spencer arrived a few minutes early, ordered a coffee, and scrolled through his social media on his phone. A few minutes later Michelle, a petite woman with jet black hair, arrived. She scanned the room and saw Spencer sitting alone. Spencer looked up and Michelle met him with a big smile as she waved hello. As she got closer, she called out, "Spencer?"

"Yes," Spencer replied.

"I'm Michelle. It's very nice to meet you!"

Michelle sat down and Spencer asked if she would like a coffee.

"Yes, I'd love a small coffee. Black, please," Michelle said.

While Spencer was getting the coffee, he wondered how the conversation would go. He wondered if they had anything in common.

"So Spencer, how are you?" Michelle asked, after Spencer had returned with her coffee.

"I'm OK, I guess," Spencer said. "Just trying to figure some things out."

"I understand," said Michelle. "I guess I'm supposed to share some things about myself and Jiu-Jitsu with you, right? Where would you like me to start?"

Spencer quickly answered with, "I guess just tell me why you like Jiu-Jitsu so much."

"OK," Michelle replied. "Why do I like Jiu-Jitsu so much? Well, that's a great question. To me, Jiu-Jitsu represents empowerment. It means having control in a world that in so many ways is out of control. I guess for you to understand what I mean, I need to tell you more about myself and my story.

"I grew up in the Midwest, where life was simple. I had a great life with my mom, dad, two sisters, and a brother. I did all the normal childhood things, like Girl Scouts and church, and was involved in cheerleading and track at my school. By the time I graduated and was ready to move away to go to college I was still a bit naive, to say the least. My first year of college was pretty uneventful, but in my second year something happened that changed the course of my life forever. I went to a party at a frat house with some friends, and we all ended up drinking too much. A guy I kind of knew—I knew who he was but I didn't really know much about him—started talking to me, and we seemed to have a lot in common. I had recently become interested in Germany, and he told me that he had just returned from a semester abroad in Germany. He offered to show me his pictures from his time there, so we went up to his room to see them. As soon as we started looking at the Germany pictures he started trying to kiss me. I was surprised by this—as I said, I was very naive—and told him to stop. But he didn't stop. The more I resisted, the more forceful he became. He pinned me down and raped me. I was completely terrified and felt myself leave my body. I floated above the scene and saw it from a third-person point-of-view. When it was over I laid there motionless for hours. I was completely in shock. I don't remember how I got back to my room, but when I got there I collapsed and passed out until the next morning. When I woke up it all seemed like a bad dream. I didn't know what to do so I went to campus police and filed a complaint. They said they'd look into it but ultimately it was a he said, she said situation and since there was alcohol involved and I went to his room voluntarily nothing could be proved.

"After that I just couldn't concentrate on my classwork anymore, and my grades started slipping. I ended up dropping out of school and I got a job at a coffee shop until I could 'figure out what I wanted to do with my life.'"

"That's terrible," said Spencer. "I'm sorry that happened to you."

"Thanks," Michelle said. "So this temporary plan turned into three years, and then one day a guy walked in who I thought was the answer to all my prayers. He was handsome, polite, and rich. I'd like to say the money didn't matter, but it did. I didn't want to struggle anymore. I wanted some security in my life. We dated for five wonderful months and then he asked me to marry him. It was like a fairy tale. I thought my life was finally going to be the life I had dreamed of. But about six months after we were married, the abuse started. First came little things. He started insulting me and saying mean things to me. Over the next several months it escalated into full-blown physical abuse. I had my nose and my arm broken, not to mention a ton of bruises and sprains. Every time it happened he'd come back and plead for forgiveness, saying he'd never do it again.

"Around this same time I found out I was pregnant. I started thinking about leaving my husband but I had no idea where I'd go, what I'd do, or how I'd care for my baby and make a living. So I stayed. We had a beautiful baby girl. By this point, though, he'd stopped apologizing for the abuse. He told me that if I ever left him, he'd kill me and the baby. I felt trapped, hopeless. I got depressed and felt that I would never get out." Michelle paused. She seemed to be fighting back tears.

"Are you OK?" Spencer asked.

"Yes," Michelle responded. "Just give me a minute." Then she collected herself and continued. "A year later I was pregnant again. I felt numb. I was just going through the motions of living, but I wasn't really alive. When our second daughter was born, though, I realized that I had to do something. I couldn't live like this anymore. The girls are what gave me the strength to think about leaving, and to plan my escape.

"After several weeks of planning, I was ready. After my husband left for work one day I gathered the girls and went to a battered women's shelter. It took a lot of courage, but it felt great going to the shelter. I felt hope for the first time in years. Unfortunately, though, things didn't go so well from there. One evening, after we'd been at the shelter for about three weeks, my husband barged into the facility with a gun in his hand. He went from room to room looking for me. When he finally found me, he shot me three times. I was rushed to the hospital while he was arrested. After being operated on for hours I woke up. I could not believe I was alive and all I could think about was my girls. Luckily, though, my husband had directed all of his anger on me, and my girls were safe. The doctors said it was a miracle that none of the shots hit any major organs or blood vessels. After a long recovery and rehab, I returned to the shelter.

"Back at the shelter I met a woman named Lacey, who was a teacher and volunteered there on her off time, helping women get back on their feet. In fact, I believe you're going to speak with her, too. She's a student at the Academy. Anyway, she introduced me to Jiu-Jitsu. I was very apprehensive at first, but with a little prodding I went to my first class. That was three years ago, and I can honestly say that Jiu-Jitsu has been the best thing in the world for me. I can't imagine not having it in my life. I started off by telling you that it represents empowerment to me. It represents empowerment and so much more. For so much of my life I felt that I needed to be, act, or look a certain way to be accepted. With Jiu-Jitsu I can just be me. And that's so powerful! There's a quote by Jennifer Gay, founder of *She-Jitsu*, that says, 'I never thought I'd find a place that encourages no makeup, requires no shoes. I don't have to fix my hair. No one judges me by my outfit. When I step on the mat, I feel equal in a way I've never felt before Jiu-Jitsu.' This really sums it up for me. I can just be me. I want to give my girls this gift so I have them in Jiu-Jitsu too, now. I work at a bank and volunteer at the same shelter I was at. I want to make a difference in women's lives, just like Lacey did in mine. For me Jiu-Jitsu is the most powerful tool to help people heal, grow, and be empowered."

Spencer noticed the smile on Michelle's face, and could tell that this was not a forced smile like she'd had to do for so much of her life: this was a smile of a truly happy and empowered person. This made him feel really happy for her. He thanked her for sharing her story with him. He knew that the next time he saw her on the mat he would relate to her in a whole new way.

"When you can't control what's happening, challenge yourself to control how you respond to what's happening. That's where your power resides."

—Anonymous

Chapter
FOUR

Juan

Later that afternoon Spencer was to meet Juan. Because Professor Johnson knew it was Spencer's day off work, he had scheduled two meetings for the same day. He and Juan were going to be meeting at a local park. He knew that Juan helped out with the kids classes at the Academy, but that was it.

As Spencer walked through the park toward the pavilion where they were to meet, he noticed what an absolutely beautiful day it was. He didn't always notice, or appreciate, when the days were beautiful, but today, for some reason, he did. He saw a young man, really more like an older boy, sitting on a bench at the pavilion. The young man stood up and extended his hand.

"Hello, my name is Juan. Nice to meet you," the young man said, with a noticeable Spanish accent.

"Nice to meet you, too. I'm Spencer."

"Isn't it a beautiful day?" Juan asked.

"Funny, I was just thinking that as I walked through the park," Spencer replied.

After a bit if small talk, Juan shared his story.

"I'm originally from Tijuana, Mexico. My family was extremely poor and the conditions were hard, but I always felt happy and blessed there.

"When I was twelve years old my mother got remarried, and we moved to the USA. As you might imagine, this move came with a lot of challenges for me. English was not my first language, and I struggled a lot in the first few years just trying to communicate. Since I was from a whole different country, some people were pretty cool to me but there were several who were very mean to me. I got bullied a lot, both physically and verbally. I was called names like 'beaner' and 'spick,' which really hurt me a lot. I struggled a lot with my self-esteem, and it was a very depressing time for me. I was really torn inside. I was happy that my mom had remarried and started a new life, but every day was a struggle for me because of the bullying. I could tell you many stories of specific incidents, but one that sticks out is when an older kid, Burton Todd, made me give him my lunch money. I was so embarrassed but I was too scared to do anything. I gave him my lunch money and then I got on my bike to ride away, but Burton ran alongside me thumping my head with his fingers over and over while saying, 'Go back to Mexico. You don't belong here.' You can't imagine the humiliation I felt."

"That's terrible, Juan," Spencer said.

Juan continued, "Fortunately, one day our school had a community festival. The festival included various booths for businesses around the city. One of the booths was for the Academy, and they offered a demonstration of Jiu-Jitsu. When I saw Jiu-Jitsu in action during this demonstration, I was blown away. I had never seen anything like it before, and I was totally intrigued. I knew right away that I had to do this. I begged my mom to let me take classes, and even offered to mow lawns or whatever I needed to do in order to get the money. She agreed to go with me and let me try out a class.

"That first class was incredible for me. It was completely life-changing. Professor was so calm and patient, and really knew how to break down the information so that everyone understood it. Before long I was going to every class available. I just couldn't get enough. Over time I started feeling more confident with myself, and I believe it showed in the way I carried myself. I didn't want to have to use what I'd learned, but I knew that if things turned physical I could take care of myself.

"One time, though, I did have to use it. This guy kept calling me names, and I just kept walking, trying to ignore him. Eventually he stepped in front of me and blocked my path. Then he pushed me in the chest and asked what I was going to do about it. I asked him politely to please leave me alone and let me get by. He started laughing and put his finger in my face and again asked, 'What are you going to do about it?' For a second time I asked him to please leave me alone. I told him that I didn't want any trouble, and I didn't want to fight. With that, he pushed me again in the chest. I immediately moved into a double leg takedown, and put him on the ground. I stepped across and mounted him and controlled the position, not allowing him to escape. He thrashed around wildly for a few minutes until he started to exhaust himself and realize that he was not getting out. At this point I asked him if he wanted to keep doing this. I even feinted a few punches toward his face, just to let him know that I could pound on him if I wanted to. He asked me to let him up and I did. I told him, 'I need you to leave me alone from now on.' He didn't say anything and walked off. From that day forward I never had any trouble with him or anybody else. I even had several people come up to me afterwards and say how impressed they were with my skills, and ask where I had learned to handle myself. I told them about the Academy and several of them ended up coming and training, and we became friends.

"I eventually asked Professor if I could help with the kids classes. He was happy to let me help and I started assisting with those classes. Now I often teach them by myself. I love teaching the kids! I'm able to really help them understand the techniques and, even more than that, I'm helping them to be empowered and ready in case they ever get bullied.

"Jiu-Jitsu has been a lifesaver for me. It has helped me completely change my life. I am confident now and I have a lot of friends. Even though my English isn't perfect yet, I don't worry so much about it now. I do the best I can and continue to practice and develop my language skills. Jiu-Jitsu taught me that you don't have to be perfect. You just need to continue to grow and learn and move forward, and stay calm even when you're facing challenges. I can't imagine my life without Jiu-Jitsu in it.

"Professor really took me under his wing and helped me so much. Between you and me, I think I remind him of himself when he was young.

"The acceptance I found on the mat has been so freeing. We are a family and Jiu-Jitsu is what binds us all together. It doesn't matter where we're from or what we do when we're together on the mat."

"Wow, you've really been through a lot," Spencer said.

"Yes," Juan said, "but because of Jiu-Jitsu, my life has never been better."

After the two said their goodbyes, Spencer walked back to his car. As he walked back through the park he played the conversation over in his mind. He couldn't help being impressed by what Juan had been through and overcome, and how Jiu-Jitsu had changed his life so much.

Later that night, as he lay in bed, Spencer continued thinking about Juan, Michelle, and Michael's stories.

"In the middle of difficulty lies opportunity."

—Albert Einstein

Chapter
FIVE

Charles

The next morning Spencer went for a short walk. He replayed Juan's story in his head. How hard it must have been, he thought, for Juan to come here and experience what he experienced. It made him feel good that Juan had found Jiu-Jitsu, and the Academy, and that he was making a great life for himself.

Spencer was to have his next meeting—with a man named Charles—later that morning. As with the others he didn't know much about Charles, except that Charles trained Jiu-Jitsu. Spencer was looking forward to hearing another person's story, but he was a bit confused by the designated meeting place. They were to meet at a church, and Spencer wasn't sure why they were meeting there.

Spencer arrived at the church at the arranged time. Stepping inside he spotted some chairs at the front of the outer room, just beyond the front door. He sat in the first one and waited, and two minutes later Charles walked in. When Charles walked in the first thing Spencer noticed was Charles's stature, and the way he carried himself. He had a fairly muscular build, and he carried himself in a way that seemed to say that he was ready for anything that might happen in any situation. It wasn't so much that he seemed "keyed up"; it was more like a quiet confidence.

Charles said hello, and the two shook hands. Spencer noticed that Charles had a very firm handshake and a big, inviting smile. He also had kind, caring eyes. The two spoke for a bit and then Charles said, "I'd like to share my story with you Spencer, if you'd like to hear it."

"Yes," Spencer replied. "Please do."

"OK, so I grew up in the south side of Chicago. My dad left when I was two, so I never really knew him. My mom did the best she could, but times were tough. She worked three jobs to support me and my two sisters. Because she was always working, she wasn't around much of the time. My older sister tried to pick up the slack, but she was just two years older than me. Even though she tried, I didn't respect her the same way I respected my mom.

"As a young African American boy living in the projects, things were not easy. As you can imagine there was a lot of violence, and I lived in fear most of the time. There was a lot of pressure to join a gang and, though I resisted for a number of years, I eventually went that route. It's not like I set out to be a gangbanger or anything, I just didn't see a whole lot of options when it came to being safe. You were either with them or not, and being with them meant protection, money, and a sense of belonging to a group. There's a lot of pull towards gangs because of these reasons.

"I hung with the gang for four years, and during that time I was involved in most of the things you associate gangs with, namely all kinds of criminal activity and violence. I didn't really want to be doing these things but I felt that it was the hand that I had been dealt, and on some level I just accepted it as 'the way it is.'

"One night some other gang members and myself were involved in an altercation with a rival gang. Things got heated, and bullets started flying. I felt a sharp jolt in my side and I fell to the ground. At first I didn't realize what had happened, but then it dawned on me that I had been shot. There were sirens in the distance that were coming closer, and the other gang members quickly ran away. I remember thinking, 'Where are you going? Don't leave me here to die.' A police car came to a screeching halt and an officer came over to me. He yelled for his partner to call for an ambulance. I woke up in the hospital and my first thought was, 'I'm alive.' I said it over and over to myself, 'I'm alive, I'm alive, I'm alive.'

"I had been in the hospital for a while when one day a nurse came in and started talking to me. Her name was Heather and she told me that she had been working in the ER the night that I was brought in. She said that I kept saying 'I don't want to die. I don't want to die. Please don't let me die!' I didn't remember this and was intrigued and a little embarrassed about it. She then told me that there was something about me. She had seen many gangbangers come in to the ER shot or stabbed, but there was something about me that made her want to follow up and see how I was doing. She came back the next day and then again every day I was in the hospital. Before I was discharged, she gave me a Bible and told me about a community center that had recently opened up and that was run by the pastor of her church. She told me that I should check it out. Before all of this happened I would never have considered going to the center, especially since it was run by a pastor, but because she had been so kind to me, and because I had almost died, I was in a place in my head where it didn't seem that crazy.

"The day after I was discharged I went to visit the center. I met the pastor, whose name was Jonathon Evens. He was a very interesting man and he told me about all the great things they were doing at the center. He told me that their mission and hope was to save kids from joining gangs, and to give them a healthy alternative in their community. Again, at any other time in my life, I would have seen this as a bunch of do-gooders trying to change something they didn't understand, something that they could never change. But it was different, now. I felt myself drawn to this cause and this mission. Something inside me made me feel that this was something good: that it was a noble and worthwhile thing to do. As I spent more time with the pastor I found out that he had lost his father in a gang-related shooting many years ago. I became a volunteer for the center and started seeing lives change through the work of the center. I saw over and over the power of redemption when people are given a real chance, when they're encouraged and believed in and are involved in healthy, positive activities. I can't even begin to tell you what a life-altering experience this was for me.

"After about a year, something wonderful happened. I had been working at a convenience store and Pastor Jonathan asked if I would be interested in working full-time at the center. He said that they had received some extra funding and grants which made it possible for them to hire me on, if I was interested. I jumped at the opportunity and started working full-time at the center the next day.

"One of the missions of the center is to help kids complete their GEDs. I felt like I would be a hypocrite if I didn't do this, too, so I worked on and finished my GED. After that I enrolled in community college, and after a few years I completed my AS degree. I didn't stop there, though. I kept on going, and eventually I completed my BSN, and an MS degree in theology.

"During this time a man came to visit the center and wanted to discuss teaching martial arts at the center. Specifically, he wanted to teach Brazilian Jiu-Jitsu. At first we didn't know what BJJ was. Pastor Jonathon had boxed years back, and a few other volunteers had done Karate in the past. We liked the idea of offering martial arts, and after we understood what Brazilian Jiu-Jitsu was we decided it would be a perfect fit. I was still working on my education and was now enrolled in a PhD program for theology and ministry. I dabbled in BJJ and really liked it, and because of the demands of working full-time and the rigors of the PhD program it was truly a Godsend for me as far as giving me balance in my life. But it was also a challenge. When I was on the mat I learned a huge and valuable lesson about myself. Even though I had become a much calmer and more loving person overall, when I rolled I would easily become triggered. Since I had been used to being aggressive in the past, I would find myself feeling aggressive and even kind of angry when rolling. I spoke with the instructor about this, and we ended up having several discussions about it. I had to learn to relate to and enjoy BJJ on a whole new level: a level of mutual respect, admiration for my training partners, and a desire for them to grow and develop, as opposed to me thinking about 'winning' or thinking of our training as a fight. This took a while but I did learn to master myself, and I grew to love BJJ on so many levels. Eventually, after I completed my doctorate, I was offered a job here in Seleno. I would be pastoring my own congregation. I decided to make the move and one part I forgot to mention is that Heather, the ER nurse I had met years back when I was in the hospital, well… she became my wife. We got married after I completed my PhD, and we moved down here to Seleno."

"Wow," said Spencer, "what an amazing story."

"It's not over yet," said Charles. "The cool thing is that when we were driving our moving truck into town, we spotted a sign for the Seleno BJJ Academy. The day after we moved in I went to visit the school and met Professor Johnson. What an amazing man he is. I started classes the following week and it has been amazing. I have learned and grown so much, and have introduced my congregation to the merits of BJJ. Now many of them are students at the Academy too! We actually have a small outreach ministry designed around BJJ. We have been able to help people turn their lives around through the power of BJJ and the redemption of Christ Jesus.

"I am amazed every day by how BJJ can affect people's lives in such meaningful and powerful ways. I am eternally grateful for being able to turn my life around, and supremely grateful for BJJ and the impact it has had on my life and my development as a person."

Spencer was amazed by Charles's story. He couldn't believe how much Charles had been through. He was starting to realize that there was so much more to people than what he thought he knew.

The rest of the afternoon and evening, while driving at his Uber job, Spencer found himself thinking about the stories he had heard in the last few days. He felt a stirring in his heart and mind from the connections he had made and the stories he had heard.

"What seems to us as bitter trials are often blessings in disguise."

—Oscar Wilde

Chapter
SIX

Josh

The next morning Spencer started his Uber shift early. He usually did a few morning shifts each week to change things up. It added variety to his week, and it also freed up some of his evenings. That afternoon he was to meet up with a guy named Josh at a local gym. All he knew about Josh was that he was a personal trainer.

Spencer walked into the gym at the designated time, and immediately noticed how busy it was. He went to the check-in desk and asked for Josh. A college-aged girl with a very lively and upbeat personality told him that Josh would be out in a moment.

Josh appeared moments later and greeted Spencer. He looked like the proverbial "golden boy": he was tall, with a perfectly tanned body and wavy blond hair. It was obvious from his build that he worked out a lot. Spencer quickly found himself judging Josh, thinking that he must have an easy life.

Josh suggested that they go to his office, where it was quieter. When they reached Josh's office they both sat down, and Josh started the conversation.

"I saw you at the Academy last week, and I was planning on saying hello, but my sister was in a play at her school and I had to rush off to make it there."

"No worries," Spencer said. "You're a personal trainer, right?"

"Yes," Josh said. "I'll tell you all about that in a

minute, but first: How are you enjoying the training so far at the Academy?"

Spencer reluctantly shared, "Well, I'm actually struggling a bit. That's why Professor Johnson thought it would be good for me to talk with you. I'm speaking with some others from the Academy, too."

"Yes," Josh replied, "he told me a little bit about it, but I wanted to hear from you what your thoughts are. What are you struggling with the most?"

Spencer hesitated, then said, "Well… it's not easy for me to say this, but I just feel like everyone else has it easier than me, in a lot of ways. I feel like the techniques and moves come easier to most people. Even more than that, I feel like my life is hard and that that makes it harder for me to progress on the mat. I feel like people's lives are easier and so they are able to focus and concentrate on Jiu-Jitsu more than me, and because of that they make better progress than me."

"OK," Josh said, "thanks for sharing that with me. I can understand how hard it must be to discuss it, and I appreciate your willingness to talk to me.

"I want to share my situation with you," Josh continued. "There are some things that you aren't aware of that I'd like for you to know about. On the surface it appears that I'm a confident, self-assured 'personal trainer guy' who has it all together. And yes, I am very proud of who

I am today. But deep inside I struggle with a lot of things. I have actually struggled with learning disabilities my whole life. For many years I thought I was just dumber than everyone else. I couldn't learn like everyone else did, and I assumed that I was stupid. I actually started lifting weights to build my body as a way of compensating for my lack of smarts. I thought that if I could at least build a great physique then people would see me for that and not notice how dumb I was. After working out for years and building a pretty decent body, I decided I'd like to help other people by becoming a personal trainer. But my confidence was terrible, and I let self-doubt hold me back from pursuing that goal for a long time."

"Wow," Spencer said. "I'm very surprised to hear that."

Josh went on: "When I met the girl who would eventually become my girlfriend, I was really worried that she would realize how dumb I was. Every day I was with her I wondered if that day would be the day she would figure it out and dump me. But as it turned out, she was getting her degree in special education. She was learning all about learning difficulties, challenges, and disabilities. When I finally felt comfortable enough with her to tell her about my situation, she was very understanding. She reassured me and educated me about the fact that I was not dumb, I just didn't learn in the same manner that other people did.

"That day was the best day of my life. It changed everything. So many areas of my life had been affected by this. I had dreamed of becoming a doctor when I was younger, but I knew that meant going to medical school and there was no way I could ever make it through that. By this point I had also started training Jiu-Jitsu, but had struggled a lot with learning it. Professor Johnson does a great job of using visual, auditory, and kinesthetic learning methods with his teaching. This is really great because most people are dominant in one learning style, and learn best through that mode. By incorporating all three learning channels it increases the likelihood of students learning the material thoroughly. But because of my learning disability, I still struggled a lot. I would see a move demonstrated and hear the explanation, and it would be like I was hearing it in a foreign language. That's a slight exaggeration, but it's not that far off from what I was experiencing. I got very little out of seeing and hearing the information. My condition primarily affects visual processing, but I also have sensory issues that affect my ability to take in information auditorily. I would have to have Professor physically put me in the position and go through it with me, in both roles, for several minutes for me to grasp it. As you can imagine this was hard for him to do during group classes, so I started taking privates for this. I made progress and absolutely loved Jiu-Jitsu, but I was now faced with a dilemma. Was I going to keep doing Jiu-Jitsu only through privates, or was I going to go to the group classes and continue to feel dumb and worry about what people thought about me? I was very close to quitting Jiu-Jitsu when my girlfriend helped me understand about learning disabilities and, like I said, it changed everything. I realized that I wasn't dumb and that I just learned differently than other people. She helped me understand that it was nothing to be ashamed of. It opened me up to the possibility of adapting myself to the group classes. This meant finding the courage to first talk to Professor about it and then to be open about it in class and trust that the others would accept me the way I was. So I took a leap of faith and did just that. Professor was completely understanding and already knew something was going on with me, but felt that I would come to him when I was ready. He asked me what I wanted to do as far as the class was concerned and I told him that, as uncomfortable as it would be, I would like to tell everyone about what was going on with me. So at the start of class one night he gave me some time, and while we were all lined up I told everyone about my situation."

"Aw, man," Spencer said. "How did that go?"

Josh grinned. "Well, you know what?" he said. "It went great! I definitely had to get out of my comfort zone, but the others in the class were awesome! They embraced me on a whole new level, and accepted me for who I am. They were actually eager to partner with me and help in any way that they could. Professor made a point to partner me with more advanced students, and actually gave us extra time when drilling the techniques. The advanced students already knew the next move we would be covering, so it was OK for us to take extra time and move on when I was ready. This slight modification worked wonders. I also made it a point to come to class early and stay late and get some extra drilling time in with anyone who was there. I realized that I didn't need to learn everything during actual class time: that I could pick up as much as possible during the class, but pick up even more during the time before and after by working one-on-one with another student. Class became a joy for me, because I wasn't stressing about it anymore. I was free to just have fun, go with the flow, and enjoy the incredible feeling of camaraderie with the amazing people there. I finally felt like part of the group, like part of the team.

"It's been a couple of years now, and things are truly incredible with Jiu-Jitsu! Nowadays Professor even partners me up with the new people in the fundamentals class because he knows that I know the material so well. And man, does that feel great! And you know what else? My confidence has grown so much through all of this that I've decided to become a doctor after all. I'm currently taking my prerequisite classes to get into medical school."

"Wow, man," Spencer said, "that's great! I really appreciate you sharing your story with me."

As Spencer left the gym he was filled with admiration for Josh. He was starting to realize that everyone had a story, and life was not easy for anyone.

"*A river cuts through a rock not because of its power, but because of its persistence.*"

—Anonymous

Chapter SEVEN

Lacey

The next day Spencer was meeting Lacey. He knew nothing about her. They were to meet at the same coffee shop where he had met Michael and Michelle. As he arrived and reached for the door handle to enter the shop, a woman reached for the handle at the same time.

"Oh, I'm sorry," the woman said. "Please, go ahead."

Spencer opened the door and let her go in first. They both stopped just inside and looked around, scanning the room. It finally dawned on them, at the same time, that they were there to meet each other. They looked at each other and both smiled and let out a quick chuckle.

"Spencer?" the woman asked.

"Yes," Spencer replied. "Lacey?"

"Yes! So nice to meet you," Lacey said.

The two grabbed coffees and sat down. Spencer noticed that Lacey looked like she had been through a lot. She looked good, he thought, but kind of "battle worn."

"I'm glad you had time to meet today, since it's the only available time I have all week, " Lacey said.

"Me, too," Spencer responded. "And I appreciate you agreeing to meet with me. Did Professor fill you in on why I'm speaking with people from the Academy?"

"Yes, he did," said Lacey. "And I'm happy to share some things with you about me and my situation."

"Thank you" Spencer said.

Lacey continued, "I've been a teacher for eleven years,

and I can truly say that it's been the best and the worst thing I've ever done. Maybe 'worst' is not the right word. 'Challenging' is a better word for it. It's been the best and most challenging thing I could have picked to go into. When I started eleven years ago, I was so excited. I really felt that teaching was my calling and I couldn't wait to get started. I was going to mold young people into the best versions of themselves, and help them discover and live their true potential in their lives."

Lacey stopped talking for several seconds and looked out the window. Then she continued:

"Somewhere along the way, the fire went out for me. I became overwhelmed with what I had to deal with and all the pressures of teaching. Teachers deal with so much. We have to run a classroom, which these days means managing a much larger number of students than ever before, and try to keep everyone engaged when most of them would rather just be on their iPhones playing games than learning about something they don't care about—something they don't believe is useful for their lives. We have to deal with classroom arguments, disruptive students, and frequent disrespect. We have to find ways to reach students who have a very wide range of learning styles, temperaments, attitudes, and perspectives. We are faced with smaller budgets every year, and often can't even afford the needed supplies for our classrooms. I have gone out of my own pocket many times to buy supplies. We also have to take our work home with us, and spend a great deal of time grading assignments after school hours. We have to deal with frequently-changing policies and directives from the administration, and pressure to get everything done correctly and on time, with more and more responsibilities piled on us constantly. We are very limited in our ability to discipline students, and have to worry about lawsuits for doing our jobs. We have to deal with parents who either expect us to do their job and raise the kids for them, or who get mad at us any time their kid gets into trouble. I can't tell you how many times I've had meetings with parents to discuss a child's behavior and the parents end up defending their child's terrible or inappropriate behavior and lashing out at me. Two years ago I had a student falsely accuse me of saying inappropriate things to her. Charges were actually filed. Even though I was eventually cleared, it was only after a lot of time, money, and emotional stress to me, as well as damage to my reputation."

"Wow," said Spencer, "that's terrible."

"I don't want to make it sound like it's all bad," Lacey continued. "I still believe in the power of teaching and I'm happy to be a teacher, even with all the struggles. But the thing that saved me was Jiu-Jitsu. I was so close to burning out. I felt like I had to make a change or I was going to literally have some sort of breakdown. Luckily I was in the teachers' lounge one afternoon before leaving, and I started talking to another teacher. She was excited about the Jiu-Jitsu classes her son had just started attending. She went on and on about how great the place was, and how much her son loved it. Something I haven't told you yet is that I have a son, too. He has autism and has struggled a great deal. I immediately wondered if Jiu-Jitsu was something that he could do and might enjoy.

"The next evening I took Ben to class at the Academy. Professor Johnson was great, and a younger man named Juan did such an amazing job with the kids. Ben seemed to really enjoy it, so we kept going back. He was doing so well in class and one day it occurred to me that maybe this would be good for me, too. Although I had never done anything like it before, and I hadn't done any real exercise in years, I decided to try it. I remember how nervous I was putting on my uniform and stepping out onto the mat that first time. My stomach was in knots and I was sweating a lot. I recognized a couple of people who had kids in the kids class, and said hello to them. As soon as class started my nervousness went out the window. I was completely absorbed in the class! And while the class was physically challenging for me, I had the most fun I'd had in a very long time! After that first class I was hooked. I knew this was something I wanted and needed to do all the time.

"After several weeks of training I noticed something. My stress level seemed much lower. I wasn't as keyed up and on edge. I felt calmer and more balanced. I believe this was from a combination of the endorphins being released from training and also learning to relax. This was amazing and I loved the feeling. The biggest area of my life that it impacted was my job. The same pressures were still there, but I was able to handle things much more calmly and peacefully. I encountered the problems and issues from a different perspective and more centered space. After several months this became even stronger. Because Jiu-Jitsu teaches us how to be 'calm within the chaos,' this ability and mindset carried over and allowed me to be at such a better place while doing my job. It taught me that leaving my job was not the only option. It taught me that I could stay in my current role and help students on a higher level by being an example of someone not just sharing knowledge but also modeling balance, clarity, and peace. It literally changed my life!

"After about a year of training I found out that I like the competition aspect of BJJ. It's not that I'm overly competitive in general, it's just that I find I get a lot out of pushing myself harder while working toward a goal. It doesn't matter if I win a competition or not, it's the process of working toward it and preparing myself for it that motivates me."

"That's great," said Spencer.

"Yes," Lacey said. "Without Jiu-Jitsu, there's no telling where I'd be."

Spencer thanked Lacey for sharing her story with him. As he walked out of the coffee shop he found himself reflecting on his own life. He couldn't help comparing his troubles and challenges with Lacey's, and those he had learned about in the other stories. In light of these, his own challenges seemed much smaller than they had before.

"The real voyage of discovery consists not in seeking new landscapes, but in having new eyes."

—Marcel Proust

Chapter
EIGHT

Sam
The Police Officer

Spencer was really starting to see things differently. Hearing the stories he had heard so far had given him a lot to think about. He was starting to understand more. His perspective was changing.

Spencer's next meeting was with Sam. They were to meet at noon at a café in a local bookstore. Spencer arrived early, bought a coffee, and spent a few minutes flipping through a Jiu-Jitsu magazine from the rack until he spotted Sam coming. Spencer recognized Sam from the Academy: although they had never spoken at length, they had exchanged "hellos" in passing a few times. This time was different, though. Sam was wearing a police uniform.

Spencer wasn't sure exactly how he felt about cops. He'd only had one real interaction with the police: he'd been caught shoplifting when he was twelve, and the store manager had called the police. The officer who responded sat Spencer in his cruiser and gave him a long, stern "verbal lashing," which had served as ample deterrent for Spencer, and he'd never done anything like that again. However, he knew a lot of people who didn't like the police in general.

After introductions and a few minutes of small talk, Sam shared his story.

"Spencer, I've been a cop for ten years. It's all I ever wanted to do with my life. To me, it's a calling. But you know what? It's really hard to be a cop in this current heated cultural climate. Lots of people do not trust law enforcement officers anymore, and there is constant scrutiny from the media. People like to bash the police, but they have no idea how hard it actually is for us to do our jobs effectively. There's an enormous amount of pressure on us to be perfect, and there's a lot of departmental politics that influences what we can do and how we can do it, which affects our effectiveness. Every law enforcement officer I know—or have ever met, for that matter—just wants everyone to be safe. This includes the people in his community, his family, and himself. At the end of the day we are just trying to make our community a better place to live, where people can feel safe to live their lives and be happy. You wouldn't believe some of the things I've been through—the things I've seen."

At this point Sam became silent. After a long pause, Spencer asked him, "Can you talk about some of those things?"

After another long pause, Sam continued:

"I've seen young children living in the worst conditions possible. Kids living in a meth house where they were exposed to deadly chemicals on a daily basis, where they had been wearing the same clothes for months, where they had not bathed for weeks, where they had to scrounge and fight for food with the roaches and rats all over the house, where they often had open, infected sores on their bodies, where they'd been so damaged and neglected that emotionally they seemed more like zombies than people. You could see the emotional death in their eyes.

"I've seen more domestic violence cases than anyone should ever see, or even know about. Including one where the girl had burns and bruises all over her body and her head was beaten so badly that it no longer even resembled a normal head. As you can imagine, she didn't survive.

"I've been yelled at and spit on, both literally and figuratively, more times than I can remember, all for trying to serve my community."

Spencer thought for a moment and then asked, "But what about the bad cops?"

Sam shifted his body in his seat and seemed to stiffen, slightly.

"Yes," he said, "as with all professions, there are bad seeds. A certain percentage of people in all occupations are just bad people. Law enforcement is no different. That's why we have cops that police the cops, whose job it is to find and prosecute cops that break the law. I absolutely abhor bad cops. In fact, no one hates bad cops more than good cops, because bad cops make us all look bad. They taint the public perception about the police in general, which I feel is tragic.

"On the other hand, I believe there are far fewer 'bad cops' than what the media and social media present. Most 'bad cops' are just poorly trained cops. They don't have enough tools at their disposal to be as effective as they should be. This includes psychological and physical tools. When a police officer is in the Police Academy nowadays, they have so many more areas and subjects that they have to be trained in. It's more material than ever before. For example, our society is very complex and we're still learning how to deal with this complexity. So when you think about things—let's take mental health as an example—there is so much to understand and navigate with that subject alone. Someone might say, 'My child has this mental condition. How are the cops going to handle interacting with him?' So cops are trained to handle situations such as these, which oftentimes, in my opinion, goes beyond what the scope of law enforcement should be. And because there's much more information to learn than ever before, it limits the amount of time they can spend to deeply train in any one area.

"Funding also comes into play here. For example, oftentimes the departments don't have the money for extended defense tactics training, so officers only get a brief exposure to physical defense tactics. They get exposed to it in their basic training, but often they don't get quality ongoing training. Many of these officers don't take the initiative to seek out training on their own time, so they end up relying on the tools they do have—namely tasers and firearms. Five years ago this became very clear to me: an officer I know was beaten severely by a guy on parole who was trying to steal a car. The officer's weapon jammed, and the guy attacked him and was able to take his gun away and beat him with it. The officer sustained brain damage from the incident, and was never the same.

"This incident had a major impact on me. It was then that I decided to seek out more tools and found myself at the Jiu-Jitsu school. It's the best decision I ever made."

"Why do you say that?" Spencer asked.

"Well, first of all, it has increased my confidence in dealing with physical altercations by one hundred percent. When you're more confident in this area you're able to keep much calmer emotionally during stressful situations, which has a profound impact on how you do your job. I've seen many officers become alcoholics due to the constant emotional stress they deal with. For me, being able to decrease that stress while having a physical outlet for that stress is huge. I'm also in the best shape I've been in for many years. But as great as that is, you know what's even better than that?"

Spencer shook his head.

"Not only have I become skilled and efficient in handling physical altercations, lowered my emotional stress, and am in the best shape of my life, but I've never felt so accepted and appreciated before. Doing Jiu-Jitsu, and being a part of the Jiu-Jitsu family at the Academy, has made such a deep impact on my life."

Spencer could see tears welling up in Sam's eyes as he said, "When I'm on the mat I don't have to think about all the craziness of society and all the hate directed at me. I can be relaxed, be myself, and feel connected and accepted for who I am. This acceptance, respect, love, and connectedness means the world to me, and I am so grateful for it."

Spencer felt his eyes tearing up as well. As with the previous stories shared with him, he felt much more connected to Sam now.

"I really appreciate your sharing all this with me," Spencer said. "I had no idea what police officers go through and deal with."

"My pleasure," Sam said. "Hope to see you on the mat soon."

The two said their goodbyes and Spencer turned and walked out of the bookstore, replaying Sam's story in his mind.

"Gratitude is the healthiest of all human emotions. The more you express gratitude for what you have, the more likely you will have even more to express gratitude for."

—Zig Ziglar

Chapter
NINE

Dr. Santos

After going to bed earlier than usual the night before, Spencer woke up early. He did not get up right away, though. Instead, he lay in bed for a while and let his mind wander. It had been an interesting week, and he knew he was not the same person he had been a week ago. Hearing the other students' stories had changed his perspective and had had a major impact on him. He was to have his final meeting that morning, and he was excited for it. He got out of bed, showered, and got dressed.

The meeting was to take place at a little bakery about ten minutes from Spencer's house. As Spencer entered the bakery a man waved to him to get his attention. Spencer made his way over to the table where the man was sitting, and the two shook hands.

"Please, have a seat" the man said. "My name is Luiz Santos. It's very nice to meet you."

Spencer replied with, "Nice to meet you too, Luiz."

After some small talk Luiz said, "I'm from São Paulo, Brazil. I moved here seven years ago, after I got married to an American. I was a doctor in Brazil, but here I work as a medical tech."

"Why?" Spencer asked.

"Well," Luiz replied, "when I got here to the USA and started looking into the requirements and the process of becoming an MD here, I became overwhelmed. I found out that there are thousands of foreign-trained physicians living in the United States but not practicing medicine because there are so many hurdles in the path to becoming a licensed doctor here.

"Spencer, did you know that even though the USA faces a shortage of physicians in many parts of the country, especially in specialties where foreign-trained physicians are most likely to practice, such as primary care, it is incredibly difficult to practice here as a legal immigrant?"

"No," said Spencer, "I didn't know that."

"Yes," Luiz continued. "For many years now the United States has not been training enough doctors to meet its own needs, partly because of industry-set limits on the number of medical school slots available. In fact, about one in four physicians practicing in the United States was trained abroad. This includes a large number of American citizens who could not get into medical school at home, and studied in places like the Caribbean. The biggest challenge is that an immigrant physician must secure one of the very limited slots in America's medical residency system, which is definitely the biggest hurdle for immigrant physicians. That residency, which typically involves grueling eighty-hour workweeks, is required even if a doctor previously did a residency in a country with an advanced medical system, like Britain or Japan. In fact, on average about forty percent of foreign-trained immigrant physicians who apply for residencies in the US actually get accepted into a residency program on their first try. Compare this with over ninety percent of seniors at America's mainstream medical schools."

"Wow," said Spencer, "that's a big difference."

"Yes it is, Spencer," Luiz continued. "In fact, one of my friends who moved here several years ago found that it took double the time she thought it would take to get licensed here, a process she completed while still having to work to pay for her visa, which was very expensive. She spent almost four years studying for her American license exams, gathering recommendation letters, and volunteering at a hospital in an unpaid position. During this time she supported herself by working as a nanny. After that, she spent another three years in a residency program working her tail off with eighty-hour workweeks and constant sleep deprivation. She finally finished last year, seven years after moving to the USA."

"Man," said Spencer, "that's crazy that it takes so much time and effort to be a doctor here, when you were already a doctor in Brazil."

"It's OK," Luiz replied. "I'm forty-seven years old, and the thought of having to go through all of that at this point in my life is about as appealing to me as chewing a handful of nails. I've spent years as a physician, and I helped a lot of people by doing that. At this point in my life, I'm more concerned with slowing down and contributing in different ways. But it took me a while to get to feeling like this, and Jiu-Jitsu actually helped with this."

"What do you mean?" Spencer asked.

"Well, I started Jiu-Jitsu several years ago in Brazil. I trained for about six years, until I got injured. It was a bad injury, and it took a long time to heal from it. After that I lost interest in Jiu-Jitsu. I only knew one way to train back then, and that was to go full steam ahead! I felt a lot of pressure to perform, and I was constantly frustrated, and I didn't understand about—or, for that matter, care about—going slow and being technical. You would think that, as a physician, I'd appreciate the precise and technical aspects of Jiu-Jitsu, but I just didn't. Then I moved here, and I met Professor Johnson. I met him in the grocery store, of all places. We started talking, and I instantly felt a connection. He invited me to visit the Academy, and I did. The more time I spent around him, the more I realized how different it could be. I started seeing the art in it. I had developed an interest in art over the past several years, and I started seeing the similarities between art and Jiu-Jitsu. I enjoy painting, and when I paint, I get into 'the zone.' The zone is a beautiful, peaceful state of mind, and before returning to Jiu-Jitsu art was the only place I had experienced it. After starting Jiu-Jitsu again, this time with more direction from Professor and wiser eyes and a wiser mindset, I am able to get into the zone state of mind every time I train. It's an absolutely beautiful experience. Time and space disappear, and it doesn't matter if I'm a doctor, a medical tech, or anything else. All that matters is that I'm free and at peace.

"This has had a profound effect on me and my life. It has helped me to let go of my ego and my identity being wrapped up in my being a physician. It has helped me to see that I am valuable and worthwhile just as I am. I've heard people talk like this about meditation, but it was Jiu-Jitsu that gave this to me.

"I also read that Master Kano, the founder of Judo, requested to be buried in his gi wearing his white belt. That really resonated with me. He had the white belt mindset as he was dying and starting the next phase of his journey. I feel like that, too. I have lived a lot of life and, at this point, I have come full circle and embrace the white belt mindset. Now doing Jiu-Jitsu, and helping others discover this feeling, this perspective, this way of thriving, is my mission and I can honestly say that I've never been happier. By the way, I am also talking with my daughter, who is a nurse here, and a friend of mine who is an attorney, about forming a company to help legal immigrants in the medical field succeed when they come here. This means helping them navigate the maze of the licensing process more efficiently, as well as helping those who don't want to pursue licensing find meaningful ways to use their training and experience to help others. I will, of course, share Jiu-Jitsu with all of them." With that, Luiz shared a big smile with Spencer.

"Thank you for sharing your story and perspective with me, sir. You've really given me a lot to think about," Spencer said.

"It's my pleasure," Luiz replied. "And if there's ever anything I can do for you, just let me know. See you on the mat, my friend."

"Challenge is a dragon with a gift in its mouth. Tame the dragon, and the gift is yours."

—Noela Evans

Chapter
TEN

*Coming Full Circle
with Professor Johnson*

The next day Spencer was to meet with Professor Johnson. He was excited about the meeting, and as he sipped his morning coffee he reflected on all the people he had met with over the past week: Michael, the veteran who had dealt with severe PTSD and homelessness, and who had come out the other side and was helping people in Jiu-Jitsu; Michelle, who had lived through sexual assault and the overwhelming shame that that brings, and who now touched so many other women's lives in a positive way; Juan, who immigrated to the USA from Mexico and experienced so much bullying, but who overcame this and was now positively impacting so many kids' lives; Charles, the former gang member, who not only turned his life around but was now helping people grow spiritually and become the best versions of themselves; Josh, the personal trainer who had overcome the shame that learning disabilities can bring, and was now on his way to becoming a doctor; Lacey, the teacher who had dealt with so many challenges both as a teacher and as the mother of an autistic son; Sam, the police officer who went to work every day doing his best to protect and serve the community while dealing with so much negativity and hate; and Luiz Santos, the Brazilian former doctor who, after leaning how difficult it was to transition into the medical system in the USA, learned that his occupation didn't have to be his identity, and who found a way to redefine who he was and what his mission was now.

After reflecting on all of this it occurred to Spencer that, even though all of them had very different challenges, the one thing that these people all had in common was that Jiu-Jitsu was their rock. With each of them Jiu-Jitsu had played a huge part in creating and sustaining balance and stability in their lives. It also occurred to him that these weren't just "people" to him, now: they were teammates, in Jiu-Jitsu and in life. He realized that it was his way of thinking that had made him feel separate from others. This feeling wasn't based on reality, but rather his perception of reality. He also realized that everyone has their own challenges, struggles, and issues they are dealing with in life, and that he was not special in this regard.

With this, Spencer took the last sip of his coffee and headed out to meet Professor Johnson.

When Spencer walked into the Academy, Professor Johnson was there waiting. He met Spencer with a big, warm smile and said, "It's good to see you, Spencer. Let's go into my office to talk." As they walked through the Academy toward Professor Johnson's office, Spencer noticed something. The Academy seemed different. As far as he could tell nothing had been physically altered, but for some reason the whole place felt changed.

As they sat down in the office Professor Johnson asked, "How are you doing?"

Spencer said, "Well, Professor. I'm doing really well." He then proceeded to tell Professor Johnson all about the week: the conversations he'd had with the other students, and the impact that hearing their stories had on him. He told Professor Johnson how he'd starting to see things differently, and how even the Academy itself felt different to him now.

"I'm so glad that it's been such a positive experience for you, Spencer. It really makes me happy," Professor Johnson said.

"How did you know it would have this impact on me, Professor?" Spencer asked.

"Well," replied Professor Johnson, "I didn't know that it would for sure, but I hoped that it would. Have you ever heard the expression, 'We don't see things the way they are... we see things the way *we* are?'"

"No," said Spencer.

"It's like the story of the two dogs," said Professor Johnson. "One dog goes into a room and comes out wagging his tail. Another dog goes into the same room and comes out growling. A woman watches this and she goes into the room to see what could possibly make one dog so happy and the other dog so mad. Imagine her surprise when she finds a room filled with mirrors. The happy dog found a thousand happy dogs looking back at him, while the angry dog saw a thousand angry dogs growling back at him."

"Ah," Spencer said. "I think I understand, now. I don't think I would have understood before this week."

Professor Johnson continued, "Yes, Spenser. Our beliefs and perceptions not only color our world, but actually determine our experience. If we are negative, or feel like we are victims, or like we have it harder or worse than anyone else in life, this becomes the lens through which we view the world."

"Yes," said Spencer, "that makes complete sense, Professor."

"Another story I like is the story of the seven blind mice and the elephant," Professor Johnson continued. "There are seven blind mice, and they all take turns 'identifying' an elephant, which is something they have never encountered before. The first mouse goes to the elephant and feels its side. 'It's smooth and solid, like a wall,' he thinks. 'It must be a wall.' The second mouse then goes to the elephant and feels its trunk. 'It's long and thick. It must be a giant snake,' he thinks. The third mouse goes to the elephant and feels its tusk. 'It's sharp and deadly. It must be a spear,' he thinks. The fourth mouse goes and touches one of the elephant's large legs. 'It must be a tree,' he thinks. The fifth mouse goes to the elephant and feels one of its ears. 'It feels like a fan, so it must be a fan.' The sixth mouse goes to the elephant and feels its coarse tail. 'It feels like a rope, so it must be a rope,' he thinks.

"When the sixth mouse returns, before the seventh mouse can go over to the elephant, the first six start arguing about what the creature actually is. 'It's a wall,' says the first. 'No, it's a snake,' says the second. 'No, it has to be a spear!' says the third. 'No, it can't be. It's a tree,' says the fourth. 'It's a fan!' says the fifth. 'No, no, no, it's a rope!' says the sixth.

"The seventh mouse goes over to the elephant. He starts at the leg, moves on to the tail, then the side, then the ear, then the trunk, and finally to the tusk. Using all of the information he gathered, he understands that the creature is actually an elephant. When he returns and finds the other mice arguing over what the creature is, he tells them about how all the things they felt, when put together as a whole, form an elephant.

"Spencer, Jiu-Jitsu—and life, for that matter—is like this, too. If we're only looking at part of the picture, we tend to make up our minds about something using limited perspective. When we're able to see the whole picture, it gives us a much broader and deeper understanding.

"As someone early in your Jiu-Jitsu journey, it's very

natural for you to only see part of the picture. But as you continue to grow, learn, and evolve, you will be able to see more of the whole. It's a beautiful journey, Spencer, and I hope you'll continue on it."

Spencer thought long and hard about all that he had learned. He knew that he was different, now, and that he was seeing things through a different, clearer, lens. He realized that his perspective, based on his limited understanding and perceptions, had caused him to miss the big picture. He felt a new spark within himself—a motivation to return to the mat with an open mind. He wanted more connection with the other students, and he was willing to put himself out of his comfort zone to have it.

He was so grateful to Professor Johnson and the other students who had been willing to share their stories with him. He couldn't wait to get back to his journey. He knew it would take him to new and wonderful places.

"I truly believe that everything that we do and everyone that we meet is put in our path for a purpose. There are no accidents; we're all teachers—if we're willing to pay attention to the lessons we learn, trust our positive instincts, and not be afraid to take risks or wait for some miracle to come knocking at our door."

—Marla Gibbs

Final Thoughts

I hope you enjoyed this story. I hope you identified with the characters and their journeys. In Jiu-Jitsu, it doesn't matter your race, your sex, your age, your economic situation, your occupation, or anything else. The mat is a sacred place where time stands still and all that matters is the interaction of those present. It's the perfect place for mindfulness. It's the perfect place to grow, learn, and develop. On the mat, the only person we have to be in competition with is ourselves—a competition to be better today than we were yesterday. That's it. That is all there is. You don't have to impress anyone. You just have to show up with a good attitude and the desire to train. Being around like-minded people in a positive, supportive atmosphere is the perfect environment to grow and thrive. It feeds the soul.

While we're there, though, we must remember that—like in the story—you never know what other people are going through until you hear their story. So keep an open mind, be kind to everyone (you never know what battles they are fighting), be supportive, and be willing to share your story with everyone.

In other words: drop your pebble into the water, and let the ripples spread…

I hope someday to see you on the mat.

ABOUT THE AUTHOR

MARTY JOSEY is the producer and host of the *Gracie Jiu-Jitsu Rocks!* podcast (www.GracieJiuJitsuRocks.com) and the founder of Breathing for BJJ (www.BreathingforBJJ.com). He is a former Stress Management Counselor and Life Coach for Duke University Health System's cardiac rehab and wellness program. He has an MSN degree with a specialization in Education, and is board certified in psychiatric nursing. He is also a certified Health Coach and NLP practitioner. Marty is a former Neuromuscular and Sports Massage Therapist, and owned an integrated wellness clinic for many years. He is a veteran of the U.S. Army, and served with the 3rd Armored Cavalry Regiment as a Radio Teletype Operator and a Combat Medic. He completed the Gracie Academy Instructor Certification Program (ICP) in 2011, and the Women Empowered Instructor Certification in 2013. In 2019, he won the Masters-6 World BJJ championship for his division. He lives in Durham, N.C., with his wife, Laurie, and two kids, Christian and Anna (and dog, Bambi).

Printed in Great Britain
by Amazon